SCOTT COUNTY LIBRARY SYSTEM

BEHOLD! A BABY

Stephanie Watson

illustrated by Joy Ang

BLOOMSBURY

NEW YORK   LONDON   NEW DELHI   SYDNEY

Text copyright © 2015 by Stephanie Watson
Illustrations copyright © 2015 by Joy Ang
All rights reserved. No part of this book may be reproduced or transmitted in any form
or by any means, electronic or mechanical, including photocopying, recording, or by any
information storage and retrieval system, without permission in writing from the publisher.

First published in the United States of America in June 2015
by Bloomsbury Children's Books
www.bloomsbury.com

Bloomsbury is a registered trademark of Bloomsbury Publishing Plc

For information about permission to reproduce selections from this book, write to
Permissions, Bloomsbury Children's Books, 1385 Broadway, New York, New York 10018
Bloomsbury books may be purchased for business or promotional use. For information on
bulk purchases please contact Macmillan Corporate and Premium Sales Department at
specialmarkets@macmillan.com

Library of Congress Cataloging-in-Publication Data
Watson, Stephanie Elaine.
Behold! a baby / by Stephanie Watson ; illustrated by Joy Ang.
pages   cm
Summary: A loving father reveals a baby's fantastic feats (smiling, eating a banana, babbling) that cause adults
to go insane with joy and wonder. The only audience member who remains unimpressed? His big brother.
ISBN 978-1-61963-452-7 (hardcover)
ISBN 978-1-61963-664-4 (e-book) · ISBN 978-1-61963-665-1 (e-PDF)
[1. Babies—Fiction. 2. Brothers—Fiction.] I. Ang, Joy, illustrator. II. Title.
PZ7.W3295Be 2015   [E]—dc23   2014019998

Art created digitally
Typeset in Marquee
Book design by Amanda Bartlett

Printed in China by Leo Paper Products, Heshan, Guangdong
1 3 5 7 9 10 8 6 4 2

All papers used by Bloomsbury Publishing, Inc., are natural, recyclable products
made from wood grown in well-managed forests. The manufacturing processes
conform to the environmental regulations of the country of origin.

For Eli

—S. W.

To my siblings,
Sidney & Ashley Ang

—J. A.

Step right up, folks, step right up! Come see one of the most amazing, astounding, stunning, and stupendous wonders of the world!

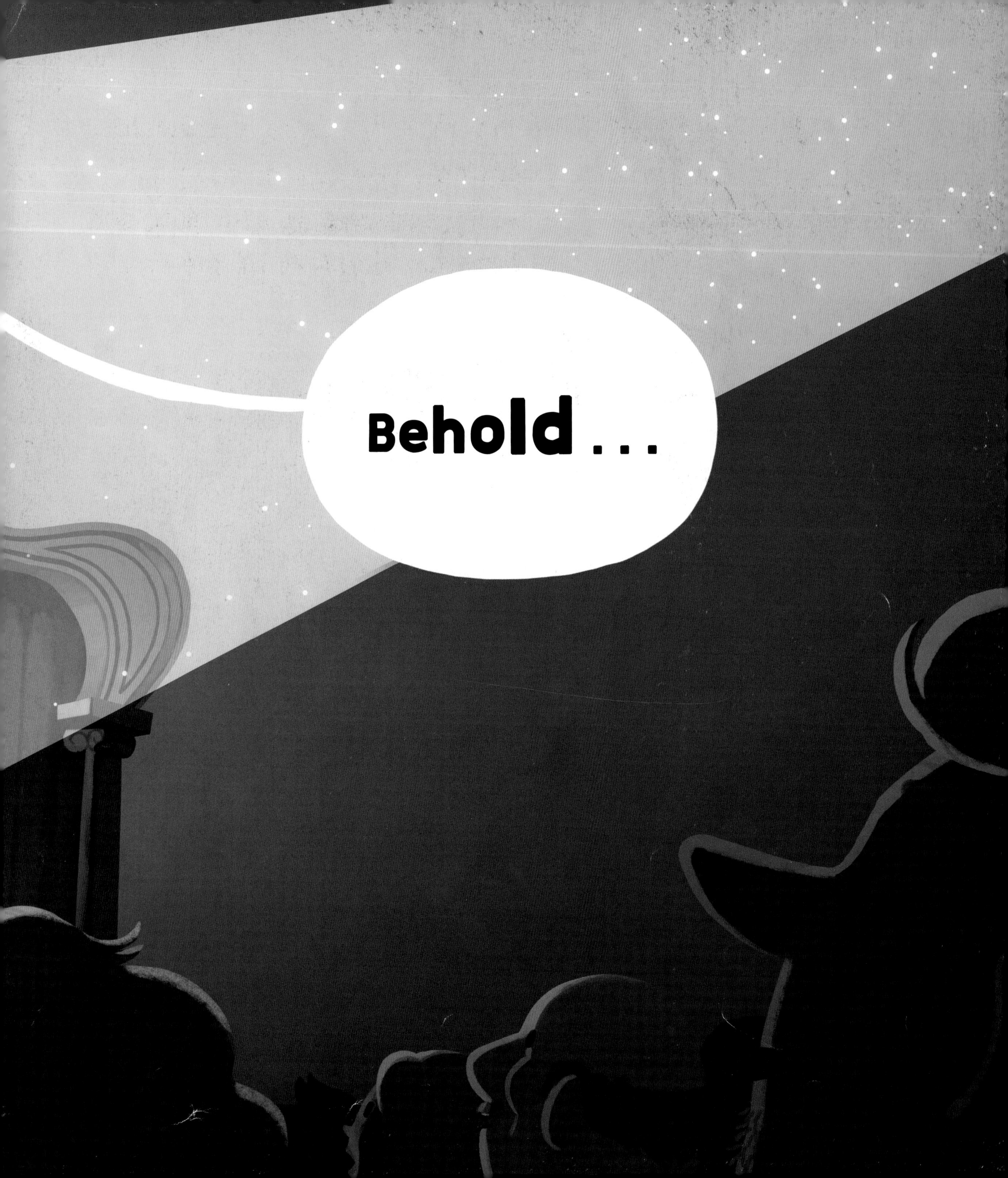
Behold . . .

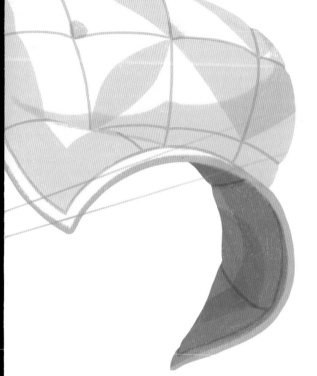

Prepare yourself, my friends, for one of the most astonishing sights that will ever pass before your eyes. Do not blink. Do not take a bathroom break. Or you may miss the fantastic phenomenon that is **THE BABY'S SMILE!**
AAAAAAAAAAH!

Next, you will see a talent so jaw-dropping, your jaw may drop when you see it. What was once impossible for the baby is now incredibly easy peasy. Feast your eyes upon the baby
EATING A BANANA!
A banana!
Look at him go!
Holy moly!

Just when you think there are no greater miracles, there is an even more electrifying spectacle to witness. I'm referring to a skill so stunning, it can cause otherwise normal adults to babble like baboons. Listen:

THE BABY SPEAKS!

Diggy dubby bubby.

Babies are boring,
Babies are boring.
Why aren't you snoring?
Babies are boring.

Diggy DUBBY bubby!
Bo babby booby!
The amazing, astounding baby is trying to tell us something. But what?
What could it mean?

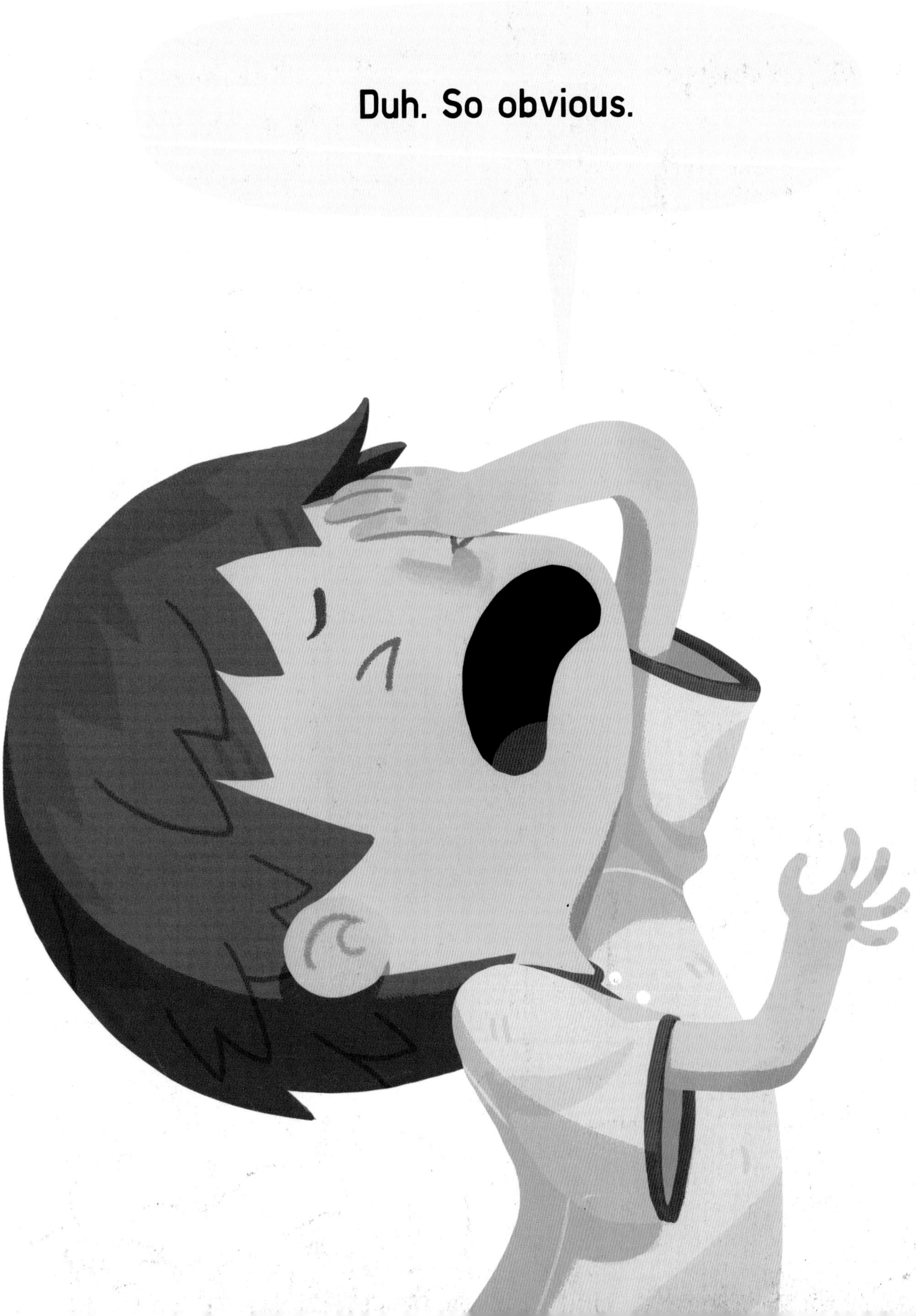
Duh. So obvious.

Unfortunately, folks, there's no one on earth who understands what this sensational baby is saying.
I DO!

You want to know the magical, mystical message? What his wise and wonderful words mean?
YES!
YES!

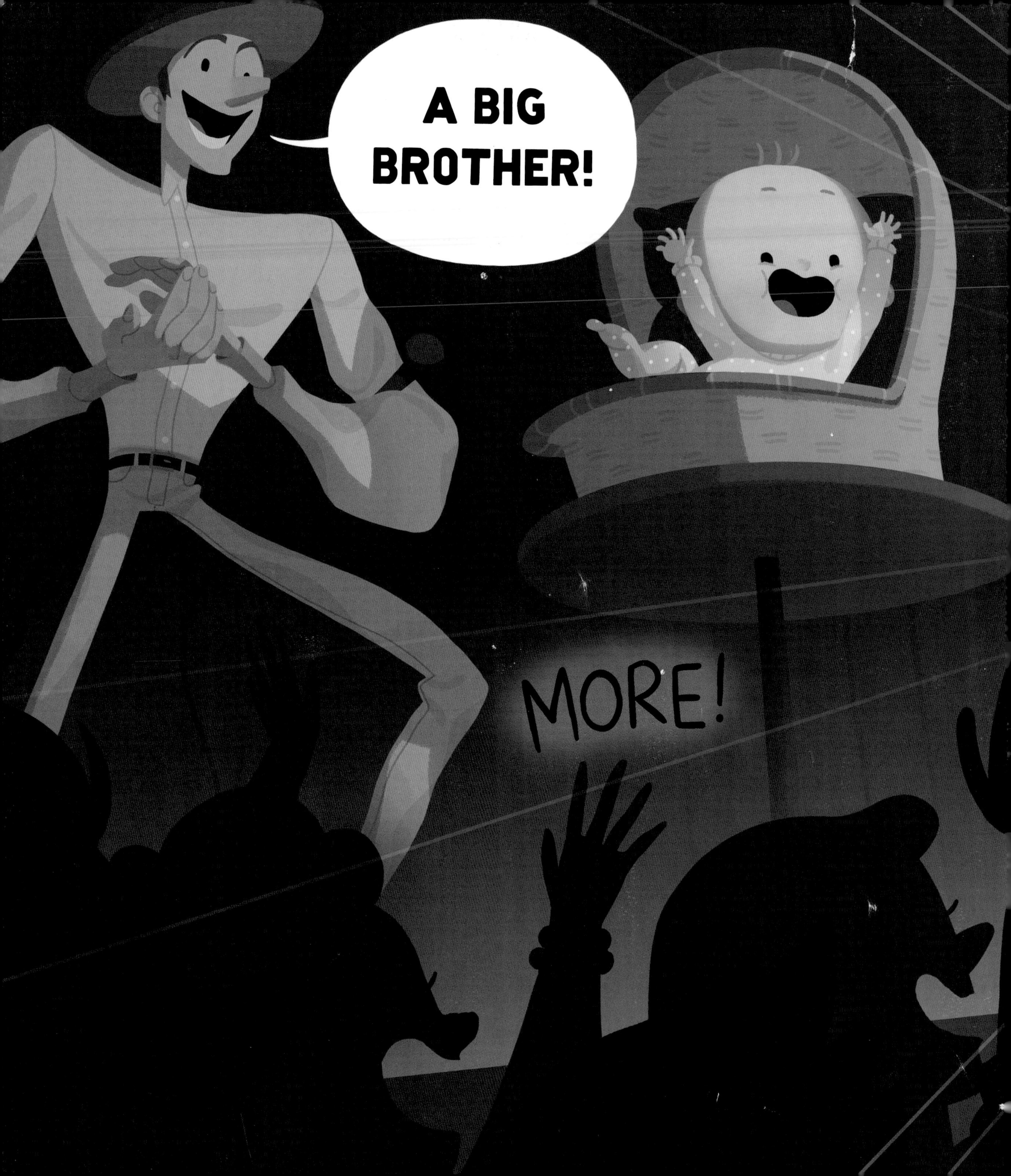
A BIG BROTHER!
MORE!

I can do lots more.

I can read him books.

I can feed him peas.

And I can make him laugh!

And for a baby brother, you're not so bad.
Bee bo?
Daga baga!
Is he asking for Daddy?

No, just a
new diaper.

Show's over, everyone. But come
back tomorrow and step right up,
step right up!